THE
SWEATY
YETI

Sink your teeth into
more Fang Gang stories . . .

My Vampire Grandad
The Headless Teacher
The Vampire Slaying Competition

THE FANG GANG
THE SWEATY YETI

Roy Apps

Illustrated by
Sumiko Shimakata

BLOOMSBURY

To Sarah Molloy – R.A.

To Sanju, Sakura and all the well-behaved
little monsters of Goolish – S.S.

First published in Great Britain in 2007 by Bloomsbury Publishing Plc,
36 Soho Square, London, W1D 3QY

Text copyright © 2007 Roy Apps
Illustrations copyright © 2007 Sumiko Shimakata

A CIP catalogue record of this book is available from the British Library
ISBN 978 0 7475 8965 5

Printed and bound in Great Britain by Clays Ltd, St Ives Plc

1 3 5 7 9 10 8 6 4 2

All papers used by Bloomsbury Publishing are natural, recyclable products
made from wood grown in well-managed forests. The manufacturing processes
conform to the environmental regulations of the country of origin.

www.bloomsbury.com
www.fanggang.net

Chapter 1

I WOKE UP AND OPENED my eyes. Another day in Goolish. I yawned, got out of bed and went across to the window. I pulled open the curtains and found myself looking into ... the scraggy and toothy face of an ugly, old vampire.

I yawned again. It was only my grandad, standing on a ladder outside my bedroom window.

'Bubbek wasnip eddy!' he said.

'Can't hear you, Grandad!' I called. 'Hold on!' I flung open the window.

Unfortunately for Grandad, his ladder was perched on the window sill.

'Aaargh!' he cried, as the ladder, with him on top of it, dropped slowly backwards towards the ground.

'Grandad!' I yelled in alarm.

I raced downstairs and out of the front door, terrified that I would find him splattered all over the garden path.

With a sigh of relief, though, I saw that the ladder had landed against the tall pine tree that fills most of Drac's Cottage's front garden. Grandad didn't look as if he was hurt, but he did have a large dollop of pigeon's poo on top of his balding head.

'Sorry, Grandad,' I said. 'I didn't realise the ladder was propped against the window. I could have killed you!'

'Phoo–ey, boy,' said Grandad with a laugh. 'It would take something more serious than

falling off the top of a ladder to kill an old vampire like me. Like a stake through the heart, or a silver bullet for example.'

'What were you doing up there?' I asked.

'Trying to fix the gutter over the door,' he replied.

The gutter right over the front door was broken and had been a problem for weeks.

Every time somebody came to the door when it was raining they would get a constant stream of cold water dripping down the back of their neck.

Last time my friend Scarlet came round, she'd really moaned about it:

'Honestly, Jonathan, it's a disgrace. I only stood on your doorstep for about thirty seconds, but my fur's soaking wet.' Scarlet's a werewolf.

There are a lot of things about Drac's Cottage that need fixing: the gas cooker that has flames about two metres high; the lights – most of

which don't work, and the loo seat which falls off the loo every time you sit on it. But then Grandad is not what you'd call handy; he is more what you'd call *toothy*.

After breakfast, the phone rang. I went out to the hall to answer it. It was Scarlet.

'Hi, Jonathan,' she said. 'Just to let you know, there's an emergency meeting of the Fang Gang in half an hour's time.'

'How can you have a meeting of the Fang Gang during the day?' I asked her. 'I mean, we're supposed to be vampires, werewolves, ghouls and zombies . . . you know, creatures of the *night*.'

'Haven't you looked outside this morning?' Scarlet asked. 'The fog's as thick as a rhinoceros hide. It's darker out there than it is on most nights of the full moon.'

I'd been so worried about Grandad falling off the ladder, I'd not really noticed the weather. I peered through the little window by the front door. It was certainly murky, but whether that was the fog outside or the dirt on the inside of the window, I really couldn't tell.

'And anyway,' Scarlet went on, 'we can't possibly meet tonight.'

'Why not?' I asked.

'Because it's the final of *The X-toplasm Factor* on TV! I'm not going to miss that, not even for an Emergency Meeting of the Fang Gang.'

Chapter 2

So, HALF AN HOUR later, I found myself walking across the foggy graveyard towards the gravedigger's hut, which is the Fang Gang's headquarters.

Once everybody was there — Scarlet, me, Griselda (who like me was a young vampire), Gory (who was a ghoul) and Crombie the Zombie — Scarlet got up and announced:

'I declare this Emergency Meeting of the Fang Gang open.'

Every meeting of the Fang Gang was an Emergency Meeting. I had once asked Scarlet why, and she had said that it would be boring just to have ordinary meetings. Having an Emergency Meeting made it sound exciting, even if there wasn't an emergency.

The meeting started OK, friendly even. There was no indication of the disaster that was to come.

'Item one,' said Scarlet. 'The Fang Gang congratulate Jonathan on growing his first fangs.'

'Here, here,' said Griselda.

'Yeah, well done,' said Gory.

'Hey, man, way cool,' said Crombie the Zombie.

It was a fortnight now since I'd grown my very first vampire fangs on the night of the full moon. And very proud I felt, too.

'Item two,' said Scarlet. 'The welcoming committee for the arrival in Goolish of Yeshe.'

'Who?' I asked.

'Yeshe!' said Griselda. 'He's the son of some friends of Scarlet's great-uncle and aunt.'

'What's he like?' I asked.

Immediately, Scarlet pulled a photograph from her pocket. It showed a spotty, hairy kind of guy, about Year Eleven, I suppose, who had obviously been startled by the flash on the photographer's camera.

'Isn't he a hunk?' gushed Griselda.

'I just can't wait to see him in the flesh,' drooled Scarlet. Which sounded just a bit scary, coming from a werewolf.

'Do you think you're his type, then?' asked Griselda.

'What do you mean?' Scarlet snapped back.

I could see we were heading for trouble, so I quickly said, 'Item three?'

'Ah, yes, item three,' said Scarlet, but not before giving Griselda a filthy look. 'Item three is . . . Tiffany Bliss.'

A shiver went down my spine. Compared to Tiffany Bliss, vampires and werewolves are about as frightening as Noddy and Big Ears. Most girls have ambitions to be ballet dancers, pop singers or Prime Ministers. Tiffany Bliss has ambitions to be a vampire slayer. I had once been in her Stake 'n' Brussels Sprouts Club, for vampire slayers. It had originally been called The Stake 'n' Garlic Club, until I had suggested that Brussels sprouts had a worse stink than garlic.

Tiffany and I had been the only members.

However, after I'd thrown her the head of her favourite teacher – which, to her credit, she'd caught first time – she'd banned me for life. I had hoped I'd heard the last of her.

'Tiffany's planning some more vampire-slaying activities,' Scarlet continued.

'How do you know?' I asked.

'She's joined Miss Dickens' Jewellery Making Club at school,' said Griselda.

'So? They make necklaces and stuff, don't they?' I replied with a shrug.

'The rest of the club are making silver necklaces, yes?' said Griselda. 'However, Tiffany is busily trying to make a silver *bullet*.'

'She must be stopped at all costs,' Scarlet added, turning to me with a steely smile. 'Jonathan, you are to resume your friendship with Tiffany and find out what she is planning.'

'But—' I protested.

'See her off for good, this time,' Gory said.

'But I don't want to resume my friendship with Tiffany!' I insisted.

Nobody was listening to me.

'All those in favour of Jonathan renewing his friendship with Tiffany, in order to find out just what she's up to, raise your hands,' ordered Scarlet.

Only one hand stayed firmly down: mine.

Chapter 3

I COULD HAVE RESIGNED from the Fang Gang there and then, but I didn't. The Fang Gang were my friends, and I knew that we vampires, werewolves, zombies and ghouls had to stick together. There is safety in numbers, after all. Besides, if Tiffany *was* planning some more vampire-slaying activities, then we all needed to know about it.

The following Monday I made a start on

becoming Tiffany's friend again. During morning break she was on her own in the corner of the playground. She is usually on her own in the playground, and the reason for this is best explained in the following really bad joke:

QUESTION: What's the difference between a mad bull and Tiffany Bliss?
ANSWER: A mad bull is likely to gore you to death. Tiffany Bliss is likely to *bore* you to death.

She goes on and on about her famous mother, who is a television journalist called Belinda Bliss.

'Hi, Tiffany!' I called.

Tiffany shot me a look, which if her eyes had been laser guns would have reduced me to a sticky pulp. Then she turned and stomped off with her nose in the air.

'Tiffany!' I shouted, running after her.

She started speeding up. Unfortunately,

because she had her nose stuck up in the air she couldn't see where she was going.

'Argh!' she yelled in pain, as she tripped over one of the many footballs that were bouncing about the playground and landed face down in a large wooden tub of pansies.

I ran over to see if any damage had been done. It was terrible! Most of the pansies had been squashed flat, but the tub was OK.

'Aw . . . Ow,' moaned Tiffany. She glowered up at me. 'Get away from me, you disgusting little person!' she snapped. I got the feeling that perhaps she hadn't really, truly forgiven me for the headless-teacher incident.

'Look,' I grovelled, 'I'm sorry about the way I chucked Mr Cheng's head at you. It *was* only a model papier mâché head. I made it in art.'

'It was awful,' said Tiffany with a shiver.

'Actually, I thought it was rather good,' I replied.

'Good? It was horrid! It made me faint!'

'I know,' I said, 'four times.'

Tiffany shuddered again.

'But I've said I'm sorry. It was just a silly practical joke. I just don't know what came over me,' I added uneasily, feeling that I might be overdoing it just a bit.

'I suppose you want me to invite you back into my Stake 'n' Brussels Sprouts Club?' said Tiffany, in a superior kind of way.

'Would you?' I asked her, struggling not to cringe too much.

'If you really want to be a vampire slayer . . .'

'Oh, but I do, I do!' I replied, my fingers crossed firmly behind my back.

'OK,' said Tiffany, 'but you'll have to do something to show how very sorry you are for making me faint like that.'

'What had you got in mind?' I asked warily.

'I can't tell you here,' whispered Tiffany. 'There are people looking at us.'

She was right. It may have been that what they found utterly interesting was the sight of me, Jonathan Leech, young vampire, talking to

Tiffany Bliss, vampire slayer. On the other hand, it may simply have been that what they found interesting was the sight of Tiffany Bliss, vampire slayer, with a dead pansy stuck to her forehead.

'Make sure you look in your work tray, before you go home tonight,' said Tiffany, with an air of mystery. 'You will find a message there.'

Sure enough, when I looked in my work tray on my way out of school, there was a sheet of pink paper carefully folded in half. I opened it up. This is what it said:

Stake 'n' Brussels Sprouts Club
Chair : Tiffany Bliss, Vice-chair : Tiffany Bliss. Secretary : Tiffany Bliss.
Treasurer : Tiffany Bliss
Meet me at the graveyard at dusk, tomorrow. And I'll explain everything to you.   T x x x

I shuddered; not at the thought of a meeting with Tiffany in a dark and gruesome grave-yard, but at the sight of those terrifying 'x's at the bottom of her note.

As I walked home from school, a steady drizzle began to fall. I quickly thrust my key into the door of Drac's Cottage, so as to avoid getting icy drips of rain down the back of my neck from the broken gutter.

Inside the cottage, it was dark and gloomy. This was partly due to the weather, but also due to the fact that it was always dark and gloomy in Drac's Cottage.

The smell of sausages sizzling on the gas stove wafted through from the kitchen. My favourite tea! Grandad cooks the tastiest sausages, made from a secret vampire recipe.

'Hi, Grandad!' I shouted, before running up the creaky wooden stairs to my room. I threw open the bedroom door and without looking flung my school bag on to the bed.

'Aargh!' shrieked a voice.

'Aargh!' I shrieked back. There was someone
– or something – in my bed. It was large. It
was hairy. And it was very, very scary. It was
also clutching Mr Chumps, my tyrannosaurus
rex.

I raced back down the stairs to the kitchen.
Grandad was standing over the cooker, his
eyes fixed on the frying pan full of sausages.

'Grandad!' I screamed. 'There's a betty in my
yed! I mean, there's a yeti in my bed!'

Chapter 4

GRANDAD PUT THE pan of sausages to one side and the sizzling subsided to a gentle bubbling.

'Did you hear what I said?' I yelled. 'There's a yeti in my bed.'

Grandad nodded. 'Yes, that's right.'

'He's in my bed,' I shouted. 'Clutching *my* Mr Chumps!'

'Your Mr Chumps?' repeated Grandad in a puzzled voice.

'Mr Chumps; my tyrannosaurus rex!' I explained.

'Strike a stake through by heart!' cried Grandad, his eyes almost popping out of his head. 'What are you doing with a dinosaur in your bedroom? I'd always thought they were extinct! You live and learn, don't you?'

'Mr Chumps is my *toy* tyrannosaurus rex,' I said crossly, 'but it's not him we're talking about, it's the yeti!'

'Yeshe,' said Grandad.

'Yes he what?'

'No,' Grandad said. 'Yeshe's the yeti's name. He's a friend of the Moons.'

Then I remembered Scarlet and Griselda's conversation about the so-called 'hunk' who was coming to stay with Scarlet and her uncle and aunt.

'Oh,' I said, nodding. 'Right.' I thought for a moment. 'Hang on! If he's staying with the Moons, what's he doing in *my* bedroom?'

'Ah,' said Grandad.

It's never a good sign when Grandad says 'ah'. It means there's something awkward or embarrassing that he doesn't really want to tell me.

'Ah,' said Grandad again. 'The thing is, the Moons haven't got a spare room.'

'*We* haven't got a spare room,' I pointed out.

'No,' Grandad agreed, 'but I offered to put Yeshe up for the Moons months ago, before you arrived to stay. And what with the excitement of you coming, I'd forgotten about

Yeshe. Still, there's a simple solution.'

'Is there?' I asked suspiciously. I knew all about Grandad's 'simple' solutions. They were usually 'simple' for him, but very difficult for everyone else.

'Yes, of course there is,' said Grandad. 'You can sleep on the sofa in the front room!'

I grabbed a couple of Grandad's sizzling sausages and was about to shove them right up his nose, when he was saved by the bell. The front doorbell. He scarpered out of the kitchen and into the hall.

I ran after him, a sausage in each hand. Grandad pulled open the front door. There, on the doorstep, stood Scarlet. She was wearing a smart pink top that was studded with sequins and new jeans that came to just below her knees. She was out of breath and panting like mad. She must have run all the way home from school to get changed and then run all the way to Drac's Cottage.

'Hi, Scarlet!' I said.

Scarlet ignored me and turning to Grandad, stammered between breaths, 'Mr Leach, is Yeshe in?'

Chapter 5

GRANDAD INVITED SCARLET in and shut the front door.

Scarlet stood there in the hall, staring at me. I was still clutching a sausage in each hand, but she didn't make any comment. She just gave me a look, which said 'So, he's holding a sausage in each hand. Well, what can you expect from a boy vampire?'

'Yeshe's in his room,' Grandad said cheerily.

'Correction. Yeshe's in *my* room,' I muttered.

'Jonathan will show you up,' said Grandad, making his way back into the kitchen.

I followed Scarlet upstairs. She pushed open the door to my room. 'Yeshe?' she called. 'Yeshe?'

I followed her in. There was no sign of Yeshe or Mr Chumps on my bed.

'He's under the bed!' exclaimed Scarlet.

Scarlet wasn't strictly right in what she said. Certainly some of Yeshe was under the bed, but he was too big for all of him to be under there. His arms and legs were sticking out.

'I think he's shy,' whispered Scarlet, with a soppy smile.

'Shy?' I said in disbelief. 'How can a hideous monster from the dark side with a reputation for eating people possibly be shy?'

At that moment the doorbell rang again.

'Well, he is,' snapped Scarlet sulkily.

'Jonathan!' called Grandad from downstairs. 'It's for you!'

I went back down the stairs.

31

There on the doorstep stood Griselda. There was something rather familiar about her. Namely, a pink top studded with sequins and new jeans that came to just below her knees.

'Hi, Jonathan!' Griselda said, with a smile. 'Is—'

'—Yeshe in?' I finished her sentence for her. 'Of course! Go on up. He's in *my* room.'

As soon as Griselda and Scarlet saw each other their cheeks both went as red as a pair of brake lights. They looked a bit like Tweedledum and Tweedledee, but given the snarls on both their faces I wasn't about to tell them so.

'What are you doing here?' Griselda asked Scarlet.

'What are *you* doing here?' Scarlet asked Griselda.

'Hello? Yeshe? Welcome to Goolish!' called Griselda.

There was a sad groan from under the bed.

'What have you said to him?' Griselda whispered to Scarlet, accusingly.

'I haven't said anything to him!' said Scarlet. 'I haven't had the chance!' She bent down towards the enormous pair of feet sticking out from under my bed. 'Yeshe . . . ?'

'Yeshe?' called Griselda.

'I was here first!' exclaimed Scarlet.

'You stay out of this!' snapped Griselda.

Oh dear. I could see that this was going to develop into a full-scale girl war.

'I will! Because I'm not staying in the same room as you a minute longer!' announced Scarlet.

'And *I'm* not staying in the same room as you a minute longer!' echoed Griselda.

'At least you agree on something,' I said. But they weren't listening. Without looking at each other, they stomped off down the stairs. I followed after them.

Griselda stormed out of the front door, slamming it behind her. Scarlet stood on the doormat. 'I'm not going to walk down the road with *her*,' she said, with a pout. 'I'm sure I could have coaxed Yeshe out from under the bed, if *she* hadn't turned up. Would you believe it, a *shy* Yeti.'

'If you can bear to take your mind off Yeshe for just a moment,' I said, 'I think you really should know what is going on in Tiffany Bliss's warped little mind.' Quickly, I told Scarlet about Tiffany's plans to meet me at the graveyard.

'Right, then,' said Scarlet, 'we'd better be careful.'

Scarlet waited until she thought Griselda had got herself a big enough start before she, too, went out and slammed the front door.

I let out a huge sigh of relief, just as Grandad appeared from the kitchen.

'Ah, Jonathan, my boy,' he said with a broad, innocent grin, 'aren't your girlfriends staying for tea?'

Chapter 6

YESHE DIDN'T APPEAR for tea.

'He's probably feeling a bit jet-lagged,' said Grandad. 'After all, he has flown here all the way from Tibet.'

At bedtime, I curled up on the old sofa in the sitting room and tried to get to sleep. I couldn't. It wasn't just that the sofa was itchy and lumpy, there was a whole lot going on in my mind. I found an old notebook and a well-chewed biro in the sideboard drawer and made a list:

Good things that happened today	Bad things that happened today
1. sausages for tea	1. Tiffany Bliss became my friend again
	2. I found a yeti in my bed
	3. girl wars
	4. I've got to sleep on the sofa
	5. maths homework
	6. ?????

I thought long and hard trying to remember a sixth bad thing that had happened today. In fact, I thought so long and so hard that in no time at all I had drifted off to sleep.

When I awoke I contented myself with the thought that whatever today brought, it couldn't be as bad as yesterday.

Which goes to show just how wrong you

can be. Even when you're a highly intelligent young vampire like me. Because before I had time to mull that pleasing thought over, I became aware that an icy winter wind was streaming through the moth-eaten curtains – along with the sun. I tumbled off the sofa and ran across to the window. It was wide open! I shut it, but the room still felt very cold.

I went out into the hall and saw that the front door was open. When I went through to the kitchen the back door and all the kitchen

windows were open too! I quickly closed the lot. Through the kitchen window I could see a hard frost on the lawn. It was the kind of weather even reindeers would find a little chilly, let alone a creature-comfort-loving young vampire like myself.

Grandad came into the kitchen.

'Did you know all the doors and windows were open?' I asked him as I tried to warm my bottom on the radiator.

Grandad nodded. 'Yeshe opened them.'

'What?'

'Well, he's a yeti. He likes the cold.'

Suddenly I became aware of a very large body filling the doorway.

'Ah, morning, Yeshe!' called Grandad cheerily.

The body stooped and then into the kitchen came Yeshe.

Yeshe looked around at the floor nervously. 'Hi!' he whispered.

'Sit down,' said Grandad. 'Breakfast is coming up. Eggs, bacon, fried bread, tomatoes and black pudding.'

As soon as Yeshe sat down, I heard the creaking of splintering wood. In turn, each of the legs of Yeshe's chair crumpled under his weight. Soon the chair – and Yeshe – were on the floor.

'Never mind!' said Grandad with a chuckle, 'it'll come in useful for firewood.'

Yeshe smiled awkwardly. He could reach the table quite well from the floor, so he sat up and began to tuck in to his breakfast.

'You may prefer to pass on the tomato sauce,' I advised Yeshe. It's always wise to avoid tomato sauce in a vampire's house. It may say 'tomato sauce' on the bottle, but you can never tell whether or not it might be congealed blood . . . at least not until you've got a mouth full of the stuff.

We ate in silence. Gradually, I became aware of a strange smell wafting through the kitchen. I thought it might be the drains. As

well as a leaky gutter and dirty windows, Drac's Cottage has blocked drains. Lots of them.

Yeshe finished his breakfast in no time. He stood up, and caught his head on the top shelf of the Welsh dresser.

Crash! went a row of plates on to the floor.

'I am sorry,' mumbled Yeshe.

'Oh, don't worry,' said Grandad cheerily. 'I can always take up pottery evening classes and make some more.'

Yeshe shuffled sadly out of the kitchen.

'How long is he staying, Grandad?' I asked.

'Oh, you know, as long as it takes,' replied Grandad.

'As long as what takes?'

'His parents have sent him to Goolish as a way of helping him make friends. As you might have noticed, he's quite shy.'

'He hid under the bed when Scarlet and Griselda came round,' I said.

'Yes,' said Grandad thoughtfully. 'Mind you, those two are a couple of pretty scary young ladies. The point is,' Grandad went on, 'his folks back in Tibet are at their wits' end. Yeshe is meant to be growing up into a huge, terrifying monster. At the moment, say his folks, he appears to be growing up into a huge, not-very-terrifying mouse. They think that a stay in England, where he can meet other young people from the dark side, will help him overcome his shyness and turn him into a scary monster.'

'And until then, I've got to sleep on the sofa?'

'That's right,' said Grandad with a smile. 'And be nice to him, so that he overcomes his shyness.'

I groaned. I was about to present a case to Grandad for Yeshe sleeping in the garden shed, when there was a clang from the letter box in the front door.

Chapter 7

IT WAS A POSTCARD from Dad:

SS *Albatross*, Antarctic Ocean
Dear Jonathan,
Your troubles are all over! Mum and I are on our way home from our Antarctic cruise! The boat is due in South America in a few days and from there I'll get the first flight back to England and come and rescue you from that gruesome town and that toothsome grandad. We'll be bringing Ant and Dec home with us – not the TV presenters, of course, but their namesakes: a couple of penguins Mum has won in a competition. When the prize was announced as 'a year's supply of penguins', she thought she'd be getting a large box of chocolate biscuits, but there you go.
See you soon! Love Dad

Jonathan Leech
Drac's Cottage
Goolish

I wondered what it would be like sharing a home not just with Mum and Dad, but with two penguins. Well, it couldn't be any worse than having to share a ramshackle cottage with a vampire grandad and a yeti.

At school I did my best to keep myself to myself. Griselda and Scarlet still weren't talking to each other. They were on either side of the classroom, *scowling* at each other.

At lunchtime I found Gory and Crombie the Zombie in the playground and put them both in the picture about Scarlet and Griselda's girl wars. I steered well clear of Tiffany, too, but she kept giving me big winks, which was her way of reminding me that we were due to meet in the graveyard at dusk that evening.

When I got home for tea, there was a note from Grandad:

Your bed's had it. Yeshe sat on it.
Gone to Mort the undertaker's to get you
a new one made up from an old coffin.
                              Grandad

There was no sign of Yeshe. I guessed he was upstairs lying on the floor under what was left of my bed. I had a quick sandwich and a glass of milk, then, closing the door of Drac's Cottage quietly behind me, I made my way up the hill to the graveyard.

The graveyard, that winter's evening, was cold, dark and lonely. Barn owls hooted mournfully in the church tower and bats flitted crazily by, brushing against my cheeks.

Suddenly, I heard an even more creepy
sound: half howl, half moan. It was coming
from behind one of the old, lopsided grave-
stones close to the church wall. I tiptoed
towards it and stopped. Peering round the side
of the gravestone I saw . . .

'Yeshe!'

'Argh!' screamed Yeshe in terror.

'It's only me, Jonathan!'

Slowly, Yeshe calmed down. He hugged his
knees close to his enormous body. He hadn't
got a coat on – just a T-shirt.

'What are you doing up here?' I asked him.

'I need cold,' said Yeshe quietly. 'Graveyard is coldest place in Goolish.'

'Reckon you're right there,' I said with a shiver.

'Best temperature? Minus ten degrees,' declared Yeshe firmly.

I shivered again.

'I want to go home,' whispered Yeshe sadly.

This was the best news I'd had in two whole days! If we could get him on the next flight back to Tibet, I could be back in my own room tomorrow.

'Everybody want rid of me,' Yeshe went on.

There was no arguing with that. 'But I can't go home!' he wailed.

My mouth went dry. 'Can't go home? Why not?'

'Because my family say they do not want mouse for a son. They want monster. And they won't have me home until I am monster!'

Hmmm . . . we may be talking the next millennium here, I thought. Paddington Bear is more of a monster than Yeshe. But on the other hand, I couldn't help feeling sorry for him. I remembered how I'd struggled to look scary, before I'd grown my full-moon fangs. I'd just been so desperate – and I wasn't a particularly shy sort of person.

At that moment I became aware of the sound of whistling coming from the road below the churchyard. It was getting louder by the second and the tune was the theme to *Buffy the Vampire Slayer*. Only one person I knew ever whistled that tune. Tiffany!

Oh no! What would she do if she caught me in the graveyard chatting with a yeti! Even if it was only a very shy one. Tiffany's shadowy form appeared behind the church gate below us. Yeshe saw it and started shaking with terror.

'Argh!' whimpered Yeshe. 'A *girl*!'

And before you could say 'abominable snowman', he'd scuttled off behind the grave-stones and round the corner of the church, like a frightened rabbit.

Chapter 8

'HI, JONATHAN,' said Tiffany. 'So you decided to come?'

'No, what you are looking at is a virtual Jonathan Leech,' I replied.

'Ha. Ha,' said Tiffany. Her nostrils were twitching. 'What's that awful smell?' she asked. She was right. There was an awful pong about the place. 'It smells like one of those posh French cheeses,' she said. 'You didn't have cheese for lunch, did you?'

'No,' I said. 'I expect it's the smell of all the dead bodies lying about. We are in the grave-yard after all.' Which lead me to my next point: 'Tiffany, why do we need to meet in the graveyard?'

'Because it is the scene of the crime,' whispered Tiffany excitedly.

'What crime?'

'I came up here on the night of the full moon looking for vampires. Well, I saw one! It was hideous! It was horrible!'

'It must have been,' I agreed, trying to put to the back of my mind the thought that the hideous, horrible vampire in question was me.

'I've drawn a kind of photofit picture of the ghastly thing,' Tiffany went on. 'Here . . .'

Tiffany unzipped the rucksack she had over her shoulder, took out a poster and unrolled it. With relief, I saw that it didn't look a bit like me.

WANTED!!

HIDEOUS, HORRIBLE VAMPIRE!!

Big fangs

Blood

Cape

Please Contact: Tiffany Bliss
Chair: the Stake 'n' Brussels Sprouts Club
and Vampire Slayer-in-Chief

'I've got lots of these printed off,' Tiffany explained, 'which is where you come in, Jonathan.'

'Me?'

'Yes! I shall need your help putting them up all over Goolish. But first of all we'll put one up on the gate. That's where I first saw the ghastly thing, after all.'

I was getting a bit fed up with Tiffany referring to me as 'the ghastly thing', but of course I couldn't say anything.

We'd just finished pinning Tiffany's poster to the church gate, when suddenly a car sped down the lane and screeched to a halt alongside us. It was Tiffany's mum's cabriolet.

'Coo-ee!' called Mrs Bliss, stepping out of the car. 'Tiffany poppet, I've brought your woolly hat. It's absolutely freezing. I don't want the cold air to get to your chest.'

Tiffany looked grumpy. I somehow don't think Goolish's ruthless vampire-slayer-in-chief was keen on being referred to as 'poppet'.

No sooner had Mrs Bliss placed a very tasteful pink woolly hat on Tiffany's head, however, than a dreadful howl filled the air. A howl I recognised as Scarlet's.

'Ooooh! What was that?' cried Mrs Bliss.

'A dreadful howl, I think,' I replied.

'Howllll!!' howled Scarlet again.

'It seems to be coming from further down the lane,' said Mrs Bliss. 'They don't call me "Braveheart Bliss" for nothing. I'm going to investigate!'

Off she strode down the lane. She was about five metres in front of the car when all of a sudden the headlights flashed on. Mrs Bliss spun round. At the same time the car began to roll down the lane towards her.

'Help!' cried Mrs Bliss. She turned and started to run down the lane.

I didn't need a mastermind to work out what had happened. The whole of the Fang Gang were up here! Scarlet had performed her scary howl, and now Gory had used his powers as a ghoul to shimmer his way into Mrs Bliss's car and had let off the handbrake.

Suddenly, Tiffany started laughing. 'Mummy's car could crash ... hee ... hee! She could be smashed to smithereens ... hee ... hee!' she giggled, brushing her hand against her neck. I was rather alarmed by Tiffany's laughter until I saw something small and dark fluttering around her collar: a bat. Griselda had used her vampire powers to transform herself and tickle Tiffany with her wings.

'Buzz off, Griselda!' I hissed, as Tiffany started to roll around in fits of laughter.

The car was getting faster and was closing the gap on Mrs Bliss with every second.

Chapter 9

'HELP HER, JONATHAN!' screamed Tiffany.

I knew very well how I could help Mrs Bliss, of course. I could think myself into my vampire personality; do a power run to catch the car and then use my incredible vampire strength to stop it from running Mrs Bliss over. But if I did that, Tiffany would know I was a vampire. On the other hand, did I want to see an innocent woman — even an innocent woman as gross as Mrs Bliss — get mown down by her own car? It was a tough call.

Oh well. I started to bend my legs and take deep breaths ready for a power run. I focused steadily on the car speeding down the lane.

Suddenly, the car stopped! Then, just as suddenly, Mrs Bliss took a great leap sideways out of its door, straight into the muddy ditch.

I ran towards the car, Tiffany close on my

heels. There standing in the lane, one massive hand on the front bonnet holding the car back, was Yeshe!

I dived into the car and pulled on the hand-brake. By the time I rolled out, Yeshe was already haring off down the lane. Mrs Bliss sat on the verge, a dazed look in her eyes, trying to get her breath back. Tiffany stood in the middle of the road gazing soppily into the distance.

'Wow!' she gasped. 'That is one fit guy! He's just saved my mum's life! Do you know him, Jonathan?'

'Sort of,' I replied, carefully. 'He . . . er . . . comes from a place where it snows a lot.'

'Like Switzerland, you mean?'

'Er . . . not exactly Switzerland.'

'I bet he's a ski instructor!'

'Er . . . I imagine he might be . . .' I said, even more carefully.

'Well, he can teach me to ski any time he likes,' said Tiffany, 'I desperately need to practise before Mummy and I go to Austria. I wonder where he's staying?'

If only you knew, I thought.

Mrs Bliss had climbed out of the ditch and was inspecting the car. 'I'm sure I left the handbrake on,' she muttered to herself. 'And even if I didn't, it doesn't explain the business with the headlights. Something very strange is going on!'

'I blame the forces of darkness!' Tiffany said.

Mrs Bliss looked closely at Tiffany. 'Maybe

there is something in this vampire business you keep going on about, poppet,' she said.

'I keep telling you, Mummy, this town is in the clutches of the dark forces of vampires, werewolves and ghouls! Jonathan believes that too, don't you, Jonathan?' Tiffany said excitedly.

'Oh yes,' I said. 'Definitely.'

'Come along, Tiffany,' said Mrs Bliss, getting into the car and starting the engine. 'We're going home. I need to get changed out of these filthy clothes! And you, Tiffany poppet, have got a big day tomorrow.'

Tiffany gave me a wink. 'It's my birthday tomorrow,' she whispered.

'Right,' I said.

Tiffany climbed into the car and Mrs Bliss sped off in the darkness down the lane towards Goolish town centre. As the sound of the car died away and once again the night fell silent, I strode back towards the graveyard.

'Gory? Scarlet? Griselda?' I yelled. 'I know you're there!'

There was a fit of giggling from the direction of the gravedigger's hut. The door edged open and out came Griselda, Scarlet and Gory.

Chapter 10

I COULDN'T SEE WHAT there was to laugh at, but I was in a minority of one.

'Oh, that was *sooo* funny, wasn't it, Scarlet,' laughed Griselda.

'Yeah!' giggled Scarlet.

Suddenly, it dawned on me. 'Hang on a moment,' I said. 'I didn't think you two were talking to each other!'

'Whatever gave you that idea?' asked Griselda in a puzzled voice.

'Yes, whatever gave you that idea?' echoed Scarlet.

'Oh, nothing,' I replied, 'just the fact that yesterday you both said you wouldn't be seen dead in the same room as each other.'

'Oh, that was yesterday,' said Scarlet with a smile.

'Yeah, yesterday,' echoed Griselda.

Girls. Honestly!

'Thanks to that hilarious piece of scaring on your part,' I said crossly, 'Mrs Bliss is now as convinced as Tiffany that vampires and other dark-side creatures exist. So both of them will be on to us now.'

'If it hadn't been for that dopey yeti getting in the way, we could've scared her off for good,' moaned Gory.

'She would've ended up a battered pulp at the bottom of the hill!' I told him.

'So?' Gory shrugged. That's the trouble with ghouls. They're just so . . . well, *ghoulish*. 'That

Yeshe's a menace,' Gory went on. 'We can't have him coming along mucking everything up each time we set up a decent bit of scaring! When's he going back to Tibet?'

I told the Fang Gang about Yeshe's shyness problem and how his family didn't want him back until he'd turned into a proper monster.

'Then we'll just have to turn him into a monster,' Scarlet declared.

'And the sooner, the better,' I said. 'That way he'll go back where he came from and I'll get my room back.'

'Well, there's no time like the present,' said Griselda. 'Let's get over to Drac's Cottage and turn Yeshe into a terrifying monster!'

As we walked through the graveyard, I said, 'Where's Crombie?'

We found him in the gravedigger's hut, asleep. 'Hi, guys,' he said with a yawn. 'Did I miss something?'

We set off again for Drac's Cottage; this time with Crombie the Zombie in tow. We had reached the church gate, when to my horror, I realised I hadn't removed Tiffany's 'Wanted' poster. The Fang Gang crowded around, reading it and shrieking with laughter.

'Who's this "hideous, horrible vampire?"' asked Scarlet, pointing at the picture.

'If you must know, it's meant to be me,' I said gloomily.

This sent them all off into fits of uncontrollable mirth again.

'No way, man!' chortled Crombie.

'You? It looks more like a cross between Shrek and Daffy Duck!' declared Gory.

'OK, OK, shut it, can't you,' I said crossly. 'I thought ghouls, zombies, vampires and were-wolves were meant to be ghoulishly grisly, not girlishly giggly. Are we going back to my grandad's cottage to turn Yeshe into a monster or not?'

Chapter 11

WHEN WE GOT back to Drac's Cottage, we found Yeshe in the kitchen. He was sitting half in and half out of the fridge, trying to cool off.

'Hello, Yeshe!' we chorused.

Yeshe cowered in the fridge.

'We've come to turn you into a real monster,' announced Griselda brightly.

Yeshe shook his head sadly. 'Me never be

monster. Me too shy. Don't like me being shy yeti. Want to be *un*-shy yeti.'

'We'll make you an *un*-shy yeti!' declared Scarlet triumphantly.

'Hey, man, what *is* that smell?' muttered Crombie.

'Crombie, be quiet!' ordered Scarlet. But I could see her nose was twitching like mad. Being a werewolf, she has a highly developed sense of smell.

Yeti was still shaking his head. 'No one like Yeshe. No one get close to Yeshe. Because I am yeti. There is nothing you can do.'

'I'm sure there is!' I said. 'The Fang Gang will think of something. We always do.'

'Hey, man, what *is* that smell?' muttered Crombie, more loudly this time.

He was right. There was a smell: the same pong I'd smelt in the graveyard earlier. Now, all the Fang Gang were sniffing and twitching their noses like a pack of police dogs.

'Yes . . . what is that *smell*?' Scarlet asked, her werewolf nose wrinkled up in disgust.

'Er . . . I think it's the drains,' I said.

'No, man, it's not drains,' said Crombie. 'It's feet. Size one hundred and thirty yeti feet.'

I moved closer – or as close as I could – to Yeshe. Crombie was right. It wouldn't be easy, but Yeshe would have to be told, and told tactfully: his feet stank. I took a deep breath. Then I wished I hadn't for the smell of Yeshe's socks was getting stronger by the minute.

'Yeshe,' I said, 'the reason no one gets close to you—' and by now the gang had moved back to the four corners of the room '—is not because you're a yeti. It's because you smell.'

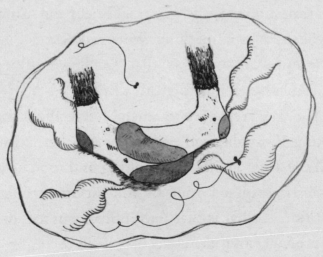

'Eh?' Yeshe looked puzzled.

'It's your socks!' Scarlet said. 'When did you last change them?'

'Change socks?' asked Yeshe with an out-raged look. 'Yeshe, he *never* change socks!'

'Well, you've got to!' I told him.

'Yeshe not changing socks!' declared Yeshe angrily. 'These my *favourite* socks! These my *lucky* socks.'

'They may be lucky for you, but they're not very lucky for anyone who has to sit next to you,' Gory said.

'You may have the body of a yeti,' said Griselda, 'but you've got the feet of a skunk!'

'See! No one like me!' muttered Yeshe. 'I go to room!'

'Yeshe! Careful!'

Too late. Yeshe's bottom had frozen in the fridge and when he got up, so did the fridge. *Crash!* went another row of plates.

Yeshe wiggled himself out of the fridge. With a sulky look, he shuffled out of the kitchen and up the stairs.

All of us laughed. All of us, that is, except Crombie. 'Hey, man! That's not nice,' he said.

Nobody said anything. Crombie's comment suddenly made me think that laughing at Yeshe hadn't been a very good thing to do. The trouble was, it had been funny at the time. Now, though, it didn't seem funny at all. We'd just egged each other on and now I felt really bad.

'Crombie's right,' I said. 'We shouldn't have laughed at him.'

'You're right,' said Griselda. 'We've got to try to help him.'

'He's lonely,' said Scarlet. 'You know how easy it is to feel alone if you're from the dark side.'

I nodded. I remembered how lonely I had been before I'd joined the Fang Gang.

'He's unhappy. And that's partly our fault,' added Griselda.

'But if he won't change his socks, what do we do . . . ?' asked Gory.

'I know!' said Scarlet. 'We could all club together and buy him some really strong anti-

perspirant perfume for his feet! You can get
really strong stuff. I've seen it advertised on
the telly! It's meant to go under your arms, I
think, but I'm sure it would work just as well
on feet. If his socks smell nice, he'll be able to
get close to people!'

'That is *such* a good idea, Scarlet!' said
Griselda. 'We could all contribute a bit of
pocket money.'

I was beginning to wonder if I didn't prefer it when Griselda and Scarlet were at each other's throats.

'Anything to help a fellow creature from the dark side,' said Scarlet.

'So . . . who's going to buy it for him?' asked Griselda.

'Not me!' chorused Gory, Scarlet and me, together.

'No way, man!' muttered Crombie.

'So embarrassing,' I agreed.

'Then we'll have to draw straws,' said Griselda.

I went and got some drinking straws from the top drawer and we snapped one of them in half. Then we took it in turns to pick one from Griselda's clenched fist.

Five seconds later, I was sitting on the floor clutching a straw that was half the length of everybody else's.

'Er . . . best of three?' I suggested weakly. But I knew I was wasting my breath.

Chapter 12

NEXT MORNING, being Saturday, I lay in for a bit. When I went downstairs, I found a postcard from Gran.

If you go down in the woods today be sure of a BIG surprise!!!

Love Gran x

Jonathan Leech
Drac's Cottage
Goolish

She was still serving time in prison on account of a spot of trolley rage in her local supermarket.

On the other side of the card was a picture of the teddy bears' picnic. Had Gran gone bonkers? No, that was silly. Gran couldn't *go* bonkers, she'd been *born* bonkers. Even so, what made her think that a terrifying young vampire like me (well, terrifying once a month on the night of the full moon, at any rate) had the slightest interest in teddy bears' picnics? It must mean something, I thought, but just what, I had no idea. And anyway, my head was filled with one dreadful thought only: I had to go to the big chemist's shop in Goolish and buy a bottle of perfume for Yeshe's feet.

I had thought that actually buying the perfume at the cash desk would be the most embarrassing part of the exercise. But just standing by the perfume section was excruciating. There were loads of girls there trying out purple lipstick and green nail varnish.

Of course, I had tried to get Scarlet or Griselda to come with me, but they had both said no.

'It's a man's perfume we need and buying it is a man's job,' Scarlet had informed me.

Eventually, though, the gang did all agree to wait for me outside the store.

In front of me were racks of women's perfumes. And they had such naff names! I picked up a bottle at random. It was called *Sinderella*. *Sinderella?* I ask you! I couldn't see Yeshe going for any of these girly smells. Somehow, I had to find the *men's* perfume.

'Hello, Jonathan!' I heard a voice behind me call.

I spun around and found myself face to face with Tiffany. She looked down at my right hand, which was still clutching the perfume bottle.

'Jonathan! How sweet of you!' Tiffany burbled with a bright smile. 'I mean, I knew you liked me, really, otherwise you wouldn't have asked to rejoin the Stake 'n' Brussels Sprouts Club. But a bottle of *Sinderella* . . . !'

It was my worst nightmare. No, it was worse than my worst nightmare. Being both stupid and soppy, Tiffany had naturally assumed that I was buying a bottle of *Sinderella* for her.

'And even though I let you know it was my birthday, I didn't really think you'd buy me a present,' she went on excitedly.

It would have been no good telling Tiffany that my real mission was to buy a bottle of antiperspirant for a sweaty yeti's feet. I had no option but to allow Tiffany to take my other

hand and lead me towards the sales counter.

'Would sir like to try it first?' asked the shop assistant.

'Oh yes!' twittered Tiffany.

Before I could stop her she'd splashed a dol-lop of *Sinderella* on to the back of my hand. It

smelt like a cross between a toilet duck and an air freshener.

I handed over all the Fang Gang's money – and most of my own pocket money – to the shop assistant. She wrapped up the bottle of *Sinderella* in a fancy little bag and gave me a soppy wink.

As Tiffany and I came out of the shop, I spied the Fang Gang lurking in the doorway of the Goolish Building Society across the street. Even from a distance, I could see that they didn't look terribly happy as they saw me mooching off down the street with Tiffany.

'Come along, Jonathan,' ordered Tiffany. 'We can put up some of those Wanted posters!'

'OK,' I sighed. Well, it seemed better than having to face the Fang Gang and explain that I'd spent all their pocket money on a bottle of *Sinderella* for Tiffany Bliss.

Chapter 13

W E PUT UP Tiffany's Wanted posters all over Goolish. We pinned them up on lamp-posts, telephone poles and boarded-up shops.

'Since that mysterious business with the car up at the graveyard, Mum's been busy drumming up support for a campaign to rid Goolish of all creatures from the dark side. That's great, isn't it?'

'Yes,' I mumbled, hoping I sounded enthusiastic. It was no use my trying to explain to Tiffany that Goolish's vampires, werewolves, ghouls and zombies were no worse than the folks from the light side. It was simply that we were, well, different.

'Our posters are just the start of a major offensive against the forces of darkness,' declared Tiffany excitedly.

As darkness began to fall, we even put one up in 'Veronica Vickers: Best for Knickers', because it was Tiffany's mum's favourite shop

and she knew Veronica Vickers quite well. And then, thankfully, Tiffany finally decided that she was cold and wanted to go home.

I watched Tiffany disappear into the darkness and then turned to stare at the Wanted poster in 'Veronica Vickers: Best for Knickers'.

Was that really what I had looked like with my fangs on the night of the full moon? It all seemed very strange. Was I a young vampire? Or was I a young boy? Was I both? I quickly turned away from 'Veronica Vickers: Best for Knickers'. It was bad enough having been seen in the perfume department; I certainly didn't want anybody catching sight of me peering into the window of a knicker shop.

As I made my way back along the seafront light flakes of snow began to fall. I sat down in one of the shelters, not really sure if I wanted to hurry back to Drac's Cottage; knowing my luck the Fang Gang would already be lying in wait for me. And even if they weren't in my room, Yeshe would be. I did the only thing I could do: I ripped one of the spare Wanted posters in half, took out my pen and made a list:

Good Stuff
1. Mum and Dad are on their way home.

Bad Stuff
1. Yeshe can't go home until he's a monster.
2. Yeshe won't become a monster until he stops being shy.
3. Yeshe won't stop being shy because he can't get close to anyone.
4. Yeshe can't get close to anyone because of his sweaty feet.
5. Yeshe won't change his socks.
6. Yeshe needs perfume.
7. I've spent the Fang Gang's pocket money on a bottle of perfume for Tiffany.
8. maths homework.

Perhaps I would get back to Drac's Cottage and find Dad waiting for me. If I did, what would I tell him? That I was a young vampire? What would he say to that? Perhaps he wouldn't want me; perhaps he'd run screaming from the cottage, leaving me here in Goolish.

I looked through the side window in the shelter at the falling snow. At least, I tried to. There was one of Tiffany's Wanted posters taped to the glass. Above it, was another Wanted poster; an official police one with a

proper photograph. I looked hard at the photograph and gulped. For the photograph was very familiar indeed. It was a photo of Gran!

HAVE YOU SEEN THIS WOMAN?

CONTACT GOOLISH POLICE.
WARNING!!!
DO NOT APPROACH THIS WOMAN!
SHE IS HIGHLY DANGEROUS!

Suddenly, I became aware of warm breath on my neck. I turned round and saw a smiling police officer standing right behind me.

'You shouldn't be out alone, young man,' said the police officer sternly. 'Not with this dangerous criminal about!' He jabbed a finger at Gran's photo. 'Nobody is safe with her around. Grievous bodily harm to a frozen turkey, that's what she was done for. It's a wicked world, eh? And now she's escaped from prison. We think she's in Goolish. She's got a grandson here in Goolish, see, so she might be hiding out with him. Pity we don't know his name or where he lives.'

The police officer looked from Gran's photo to me and back again.

'She looks a bit like you,' he said.

He stared at the poster again. 'In fact, she looks very like you. Why, you could almost be related.'

I bent my knees, took a deep breath and pushed forward. I reckoned it was time for one of my power runs.

Chapter 14

I JUST HAD TIME to hear the police officer yell:

'Oi! Come back here!'

And then I was surging my way along the seafront. As I turned to head up the hill towards Drac's Cottage, my feet slipped in the snow, but I managed to keep my balance.

By the time I passed Mort the undertaker's body-repair workshop, I knew I had left the police officer far behind. I slowed down and trotted the last few hundred metres to Drac's Cottage. It looked even more run down in the snow. The front gate was leaning over at a crazy angle and the garden fence was lying on the ground.

There was no sign of Grandad in the kitchen. But there was a postcard addressed to me, propped up on the worktop against a bottle of blood.

Venezuela, S America

Dear Jonathan

I am sorry to say that my plan to get back quickly to England to rescue you has been delayed. When we got to South America, your mum discovered that her penguins, Ant and Dec, were actually Ant and *Deb*. Deb hatched three chicks last night. Your mum needs me to stay with her and look after the baby penguins until they are big enough to travel back to England with us.

Love Dad

Jonathan Leech
Drac's Cottage
Goolish

Typical! I might have known it! You need your parents to come and rescue you and what happens? They get held up having to rear a clutch of penguin chicks!

I went upstairs to my room. There was no sign of Yeshe, just the lingering smell of his size one hundred and thirty feet. I was just about to go downstairs again when I caught sight of a note pinned to the door.

Am sorry about foots.
Have gone place I won't
be trouble no one.
Yeshe

I felt awful. I know I'd moaned about him nicking my room, but now he'd gone walkabout somewhere out there in the freezing wilds of Goolish with no food and no shelter and on a snowy night, just because the Fang Gang had complained about his socks.

Mind you, they did smell.

We had to find him! Before something bad

happened to him! But how? I had to flop down and have a think. Unfortunately, although I had my room back, I still didn't have a bed.

I went back downstairs into the front room and flopped down on the sofa. Then I flopped straight up again.

'Aargh!' I screamed as a bony fist punched my bottom.

Rising from the depths of the sofa, like the Loch Ness monster surfacing, appeared the startled figure of Gran.

'Jonathan?'

'Gran?'

'Well, of course it's me! Who did you think it was?'

Once I'd recovered from the shock, I took Gran through to the kitchen and made her a cup of tea.

'I finally made good my escape from prison, Jonathan!' she declared excitedly.

'So I see,' I commented.

'Do you want to know how I did it?'

I didn't get a chance to say no.

'As you know, I'd tried to escape in the prison laundry van, but that only took me to another prison. So, this time I hid out in the laundry van and when it arrived at the next prison, I slipped out the back doors and into the driving seat, while the driver and his mate were picking up the dirty laundry. I made straight for Goolish, stopping at a post office on the way to send you a kind of coded card to warn you I was coming. You did get it?'

I remembered the teddy bears' picnic postcard.

"'If you go down in the woods today . . . ?'"
Well, I hid up in the woods above Goolish
until dusk. I thought you might have worked
out what I was saying and come and brought
me a flask of soup or something,'

'Sorry, Gran,' I said. 'It never occurred to
me—'

'Well, I'm here now!' said Gran cheerily.

'Where's the van?' I asked.

'Your grandad's kindly driven it round to his

friends, the Moons. Millie's going to put it in the garage with the Brownies' minibus.'

'But . . . Grandad can't drive!' I said in amazement. And I knew then why the garden fence was on the ground and the gate was off its hinges.

I heard the front door click and in came Grandad. He was clutching a bag, and by the silly toothy grin he had on his face, I could see he was in one of his soppy moods.

'Did you get the van to the Moons' OK?' asked Gran.

'Yes . . . just a few dents on the way,' said Grandad. He turned to me. 'Fancy your gran turning up like this, eh, boy? Do you know, she and I haven't seen each other since your mum and dad's wedding, thirteen years ago!'

I should point out, just in case you hadn't worked it out already, that Grandad was my dad's dad; and Gran was my mum's mum.

'Such a pleasure, isn't it, Jonathan?' Grandad was saying.

I had a dreadful feeling that Grandad was

going to witter on in this vein for about a hundred hours. I was just about to open my mouth to try and shut him up, when the front-door bell rang.

Gran went pale. 'It's the police!' she whispered. 'They've come to take me back to that awful prison!'

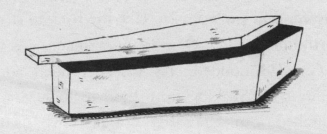

Chapter 15

AND IF BY ANY chance it's not the police, it'll be the Fang Gang come to ask me why I spent all their pocket money on perfume for Tiffany, I thought.

'You've got to hide, Esmeralda!' Grandad hissed to Gran.

'Where? You know what the police are like, they'll search everywhere!'

Grandad shook his head. 'There's one place

in Drac's Cottage they'd never dare look. Come on!'

Up the stairs we went on tiptoe to Grandad's room.

'There!' he said, pointing to his coffin with a triumphant smile.

'In there?' asked Gran in a horrified voice.

Grandad nodded. 'It's nicely padded and quite cosy.' Shaking from head to foot, Gran climbed into Grandad's coffin. 'Give us a hand, boy,' Grandad ordered.

Between us, we slipped the lid on top of the coffin. The doorbell rang again. More furiously this time.

'You go down and answer it,' he whispered.

'Me?'

'Well, I can't, can I?' said Grandad.

'Why not?' I asked.

'In case it's that young woman police officer,' explained Grandad. 'I can never see her without wanting to take a bite from her luscious neck.'

'Grandad!'

'I wouldn't be able to stop myself, you know!' said Grandad.

'All right,' I sighed. 'You get in the sitting room. And stay there!'

Gingerly, I opened the front door.

'Hello, Jonathan!' There on the doorstep stood, not the police, but Tiffany. 'Can I come in?'

'Er . . . well . . .' I knew if I said no, Tiffany would just stand there on the doorstep, ringing the bell until I changed my mind.

'I just didn't know who to turn to,' said Tiffany with a dramatic sob as I showed her through to the kitchen.

'The thing is Jonathan, it's my mum. She's gone missing,'

'What do you mean, she's gone missing?' I asked.

'She went out in the car this afternoon. All she said was she "wanted to make the most of the snow".'

'"Make the most of the snow"?'

'I don't know what she meant,' Tiffany shrugged, 'but she never came back.'

'Have you gone to the police?'

Tiffany nodded. 'They said they'd try to help, but all their officers are out looking for a highly dangerous escaped criminal. So I came to you for help. You see, I haven't got any other friends.' This was quite true, of course. 'And I didn't know who else to turn to. I'm terrified of staying in our house on my own. The police reckon this criminal on the loose is hiding out very near here.'

If only you knew just how near, I thought. 'How did you know where I lived?' I asked.

Tiffany sniffed, dabbed her eyes and then smiled. 'It was easy, really. I knew you lived with your grandad. So I looked up "Leech" in the phone book. There was only one.'

My mind was in a whirl. Why did everyone – Yeshe, the Fang Gang, Gran, Tiffany – seem to think that Drac's Cottage was some sort of hotel? More to the point, how was I to stop

Tiffany from seeing Gran or Grandad?

If she saw Gran, she would be sure to recognise her as Goolish's most wanted criminal. If she saw Grandad, she would recognise him as the toothy old vampire who had scared her and her mum at the traffic lights one night in the centre of town. Then, she would be sure to realise that I was a vampire too.

Suddenly, I heard Grandad's voice outside the kitchen door. 'Have they gone, boy?'

Then, before I could do anything to stop him, the kitchen door opened and in came Grandad.

Chapter 16

A T LEAST, I SAY Grandad came in, but for a moment I thought it was someone else. He looked completely different. For a start, he had put on a smart pair of trousers and a shirt. But the thing that was most striking was his head. Five minutes before Grandad's head had been home to a few straggly wisps of silver hair; now it boasted a full mop of luxurious, black curls. There was no way Tiffany would recognise him as the old man who had scared her at the traffic lights.

That was the good news. The bad news was that the reason for Grandad's new trousers, shirt and wig was obviously that, once again, he was in love. Grandad in love was a liability and an embarrassment.

I had just managed to hide the tumbler that contained his false fangs in the cupboard. Tiffany was looking at the rows and rows of bottles of blood lined up on the worktop. I was desperately hoping that she would assume they were all tomato ketchup bottles, when the front door bell rang.

'I'll get it!' I said. It just had to be the police, this time.

But it wasn't. There on the front doorstep, stood the Fang Gang. In a way, I think I would have preferred to have faced the police.

'You've got some explaining to do . . .'

'Where's our pocket money . . . ?'

'And where's the perfume for Yeshe's feet?'

I went out on to the doorstep and shut the door behind me. 'Shh . . . !' I said.

'I'm not shushing until I get my money back!' declared Gory.

'There's no time for that now,' I whispered. 'Tiffany's in the kitchen!'

'What!' they all chorused. 'Why?'

'It seems she's gone from being the child of a one-parent family to being the child of a no-parent family,' I explained. 'But Tiffany can take care of herself. The really worrying thing is that Yeshe has disappeared. He's upset about the way we treated him.'

'I suppose we were rather horrid,' said Griselda.

'With a bit of luck, he'll be out there tuck-
ing into Mrs Bliss,' replied Gory gleefully.

'Gory!'

'I mean, yetis are supposed to eat people,
aren't they?' Gory added.

'Gory, you're a ghoul!' snapped Griselda.

'That's right,' said Gory, with a smile.

'Look,' I said, 'if Yeshe is out all alone on a night like this, we've got to try to find him. Particularly as it was, well . . . sort of our fault in the first place that he's gone.'

'If he's still wearing those foul-smelling socks of his,' muttered Gory, 'we should be able to sniff him out.'

'Whatever,' Scarlet said. 'Jonathan's right. The important thing is to find Yeshe. 'He's frightened, lonely . . . he's lost. He's away from home in a strange country.'

'I agree,' said Griselda. 'He's a fellow creature from the dark side. He needs our help.'

'Coo-ee! Jonathan . . . ?'

The front door opened and there stood Tiffany.

Chapter 17

THERE WAS A moment's silence. I gulped.

'Er . . . Tiffany!' I exclaimed. 'Fantastic news! Look who's turned up!'

Tiffany looked less than pleased. 'Yes . . . I can see. It's the Fang Gang.'

'That's right!' I went on brightly. 'They've offered to help look for your mum.'

Tiffany looked doubtful.

'We'll need all the help we can get, if we're to find her,' I said.

Tiffany didn't look convinced. 'How do they know she's missing?' she asked suspiciously.

'Oh,' I said quickly, 'it's a major news story, what with your mum being so famous and all that.'

'Really?' asked Tiffany, a tinge of excitement in her voice.

The others waded in to back me up. I rather wish they hadn't. 'Oh yes,' Scarlet said. 'It's on all the news channels. BBC News 24.'

'And CNN . . .' said Gory.

'Al Jazeera,' added Griselda.

'Newsround,' Crombie suggested, not wanting to be left out.

'Yes, OK, she gets the idea,' I snapped.

'I'm coming with you,' announced Tiffany.

'Oh no you're not!' we chorused.

'Oh yes I am,' said Tiffany.

This was turning into a scene from a Christmas pantomime.

'But it's cold and dark out there,' I pointed out.

'That's because it's winter. And it's night time,' Tiffany explained. 'Now if you're joining us Jonathan, you'd better grab your coat.'

There was nothing else for it. I got my coat from the hall, yelled to Grandad that I was going out and trudged off down the snow-covered front path, Tiffany in front of me, the Fang Gang close behind.

I let Tiffany walk on until she was just out of earshot. Then I turned round to the Fang Gang.

'I am not going hunting for the Bliss woman!' Gory snarled.

'You don't need to,' I whispered. 'We'll split up. That way you can look for Yeshe. I quite agree with you Gory, Mrs Bliss is old enough and ugly enough to look after herself.'

'Good idea,' said Scarlet. 'Griselda and I will head up to the woods. That's the sort of place a monster from the dark side would hide out.'

Tiffany had stopped and turned round. 'Jonathan?' she called.

'I was just saying it would be a good idea if we split up,' I said. 'Better chance of finding your mum, that way. Scarlet and Griselda are

going up the hill towards the woods. You and I, Tiffany, can go down towards the town—'

'And Gory and I will just kind of hang out, man,' said Crombie.

Tiffany and I began to walk down the hill, trudging up and down every side street – Tiffany looking for her mum's car, me looking for Yeshe as well.

But we found nothing.

'It's no good. I've got this awful feeling she's been taken,' sobbed Tiffany. 'By one of those dreadful vampires or werewolves, probably.'

We walked on in silence. Then:

'Aargh!' screamed Tiffany suddenly. 'What's that?'

'Just a bat,' I sighed. Griselda was up to her old tricks again. How she thought she'd see anything in her bat form, I don't know. Everyone knows that bats can't see in the dark.

Then from behind us, further up the hill, we heard the sound of loud party music. Tiffany sniffed and started to sob.

'What's wrong?' I asked her.

'It's just . . . that sounds like my mum's favourite. She plays it all the time in the car.'

The bat swooped down again, tickling my ears. 'Griselda!' I hissed. Then the penny dropped. Griselda had appeared to try and tell me something.

'You say your mum played it all the time in her car?' I said to Tiffany. 'Perhaps that's your mum's car stereo playing now!'

We raced back up the hill in the direction the music was coming from. We slipped and slid in the snow. Twice Tiffany fell over and I had to help her up.

The music got louder all the time, but it wasn't until we were right at the top of the hill, where the road ended and the woods began, that we saw Mrs Bliss's cabriolet.

'Mummy! Mummy!' cried Tiffany, running to the car and pulling open the driver's door.

But it wasn't Mrs Bliss inside the car: it was Crombie and Gory, their eyes shut, their heads nodding and their arms waving like mad in time to the music.

'Hey, guys! Welcome to the party!' cried Crombie.

Chapter 18

THERE WAS NO SIGN of Mrs Bliss at all and Crombie and Gory said they hadn't seen her.

'Oh dear,' wailed Tiffany. 'What do we do now?'

'Follow these footprints up the hill?' suggested Scarlet.

She was pointing to a set of footprints that led from the car up the hill towards

Deadman's Wood. We followed them along a wide track that in the summer was used by the foresters' tractors and lorries. Gory was in front. He stopped suddenly and pointed down to the ground. There in the snow was another set of prints. These were large footprints; very large footprints; size one hundred and thirty yeti-type footprints.

'Eeeikk!' screamed Tiffany. 'They're the footprints of an abominable snowman! Mummy's been taken off and eaten!'

'With a bit of luck, yes,' muttered Gory under his breath.

'Shhh . . .' said Griselda. 'Listen!'

We all stood still. Flurries of wet snow dropped on to our heads from the branches above. Then:

'Help!' we heard. It was Mrs Bliss's voice, coming from further up the hill.

We trudged through the snow. Mrs Bliss kept calling and her voice kept getting louder.

Then the track opened out into a little clearing. At the edge of this clearing lay Mrs

Bliss, a pair of skis strapped to her feet. And with her, his arm supporting her shoulders, was Yeshe.

'Mummy!' cried Tiffany.

'Yeshe!' cried the rest of us.

'Tiffany poppet!' cried Mrs Bliss. 'I've been so lucky. This is the second time this week this handsome and daring young man has saved my life.'

Gory and Crombie both looked round trying to spot a handsome young man, until they realised Mrs Bliss was talking about Yeshe.

'You see, I thought I'd make the most of this snow while it lasted,' said Mrs Bliss, 'and come up to the top of the hill here to practise my skiing. I was desperate to get in good form before Tiffany and I go on our skiing holiday to Austria. I know there's a dry-ski slope a few

miles from Goolish, but whenever I've been there it's been full of common types. Coming up to the hillside here seemed such a good idea. But I hit a concealed tree stump, fell head over my skis and sprained my ankle. Then out of the trees came this wonderful young man, Yeshe!'

I could've sworn I saw Yeshe blush with pride.

'Was nothing,' he said. 'I couldn't have leave

you here, you might freezed to death!'

I heard Gory groan and mutter, 'If only!'

'We'll call an ambulance,' said Griselda, getting out her mobile. She stared at the screen and shook her head in disgust. 'I don't believe it. There's no signal up here.'

'Huh! Who needs twenty-first-century technology?' Scarlet whispered in my ear. I saw her disappear into the woods.

Next thing the air was filled with a terrifying, echoing howl.

'Aargh!' screamed Mrs Bliss.

'Aargh!' screamed Tiffany.

I recognised it straight away as Scarlet's werewolf howl.

A few seconds later, somewhere, way out on the other side of town, I guessed about where Scarlet's uncle and aunt lived, a faint howl drifted back through the air towards us, as if in answer.

'Get me out of here!' moaned Mrs Bliss.

Between us, Yeshe and I carried Mrs Bliss down the hillside. Luckily, Mrs Bliss was so

desperate to get out of the woods that it never crossed her mind to wonder how a smallish twelve-year-old boy like me had the strength to help Yeshe carry a fully grown adult all the way down the snow-covered hillside.

One thing I noticed was that out here in the cold open air, Yeshe's feet hardly smelt at all. In fact, what did smell was perfume. Unfortunately, the others noticed it too and started sniffing.

'It's my perfume,' said Tiffany with a blush. 'Jonathan bought it for me for my birthday!'

I cringed and felt Gory's, Crombie's and Scarlet's eyes all boring into me. I hadn't heard the last of it, I knew.

'Where's Griselda?' asked Tiffany suddenly.

'Oh, I expect she stopped to tie up her shoelace,' suggested Scarlet.

In fact, out of the corner of my eye I had just seen Griselda morph into her bat form again and flutter away over the trees. She and Scarlet had planned something between them, but I didn't know what.

Chapter 19

I FOUND OUT SOON enough when we reached the lane at the bottom of the woods. There waiting for us was Scarlet's great-uncle Monty. He was standing by a white van that had two very battered front wings.

'Why, look!' exclaimed Scarlet in a surprised voice which fooled no one apart from Tiffany and Mrs Bliss. 'Fancy that! It's my great-uncle Monty. He will be able to take us all down to

Goolish General Hospital in his white van!'

So Scarlet had howled a werewolf call to her great-uncle and aunt – just to make sure they were in and Griselda had flown across Goolish to tell them where we were and what the trouble was.

'Isn't that lucky, Tiffany poppet?' Mrs Bliss said.

'Yes,' said Tiffany, with a frown. She knew something weird was going on, but she didn't know just what.

Griselda stood by the van with a big smile on her face.

'Oh, hello, Griselda, did you get your shoelaces tied OK?' asked Tiffany.

Griselda looked at her as if she thought she was mad. And no wonder, for when we looked down at Griselda's feet, we saw she was wearing boots. Luckily, before Tiffany could ask any further awkward questions, Great-uncle Monty helped Yeshe and I get Mrs Bliss and Tiffany into the back of the van. It was then that I saw the telltale lettering on the driver's door:

HM Prison
Laundry Service

This was the van that Gran had escaped from prison in!

'Gotta signal! Gotta signal!' Mrs Bliss was shouting to Tiffany, excitedly, as we all climbed in the back of the van. She was busily texting on her mobile. 'I'm just going to ring round a few journalist friends. Most of them are already in Goolish, covering the story about the dangerous escaped prisoner! I'm going to let them know about this even more important story – the amazing escape of brilliant journalist Belinda Bliss from the icy jaws of death.'

Next to me, Gory sighed sadly. 'If only,' he muttered.

When we reached the hospital, the entrance to the casualty department was seething with photographers and TV crews. They took photo after photo of Mrs Bliss sitting in a wheelchair with her arm around Yeshe's waist.

'This is the young hero who saved my life!' Mrs Bliss told the reporters.

'My name it is Yeshe,' said Yeshe with a smile. 'And I am a y . . . er . . . young person from Tibet! Very happy to save this young lady life!

Mrs Bliss blushed and giggled. It was probably about a hundred years since anybody had ever referred to her as 'young'. 'I was terrified up there in the woods,' she said. 'Particularly with this dangerous escaped criminal on the loose.'

There were half a dozen or so sirens wailing behind us. I thought it was a fleet of ambulances at first, but when I turned round, I saw a whole row of police cars and vans. An officer with a megaphone leapt out of the first car.

'Freeze!' he yelled.

This was a completely unnecessary thing to say, because as it had started snowing again, all of us − apart from Yeshe − were already freezing.

Then, before you could say 'bang to rights',

two more officers had grabbed hold of Mrs
Bliss's wheelchair and heaved it into the back
of a police van.

'I'm arresting you,' the officer in charge told
Mrs Bliss, 'on suspicion of being a dangerous
escaped criminal! Sergeant Pepper, impound
her getaway vehicle!'

Another officer ran across to the prison
laundry van.

Tiffany started bawling her eyes out. 'Mummy! Mummy!'

'I'm innocent!' shouted Mrs Bliss. 'Innocent!'

'That's what they all say,' sighed the officer in charge.

What happened next I don't know, because by then I was halfway down the drive towards the hospital gates, closely followed by the rest of the Fang Gang and Great-uncle Monty. Yeshe, who didn't seem to like the police any more than the rest of us, was ahead of us with a good ten-metre start.

Chapter 20

FIFTEEN MINUTES LATER, we arrived worn out and breathless at Scarlet's place.

When we told Scarlet's great-aunt Millie what had happened, she said, 'Why didn't you use the Brownies' minibus?' Great-aunt Millie is Brown Howl leader of Goolish's Brownies.

'Didn't want to waste the petrol,' muttered Great-uncle Monty.

'None of this would have happened if you'd taken the trouble to eat Mrs Bliss in the first place,' Gory crumbled, with a cross look at Yeshe.

Yeshe's nostrils suddenly flared. He took half a step towards the startled Gory, towering over him. 'You are most gormless ghoul I ever meet!' he roared, as Gory took a step back and found himself trapped against the wall. 'I have known dung beetles with more brain than you! You from dark side, yes?'

Gory didn't move.

'I say, you from dark side, yes?' Yeshe repeat-

ed, this time even louder and more threateningly.

'Yes!' Gory said. It came out as a sort of frightened squeak.

'Then you should not be stupid enough to believe silly old lies about yetis eating man and woman. Just stories and lies put about by crazy explorer people!'

'Right!' said Scarlet. 'Just like the stupid stories about vampires turning light-side people into vampires by biting them is a load of nonsense.'

'Is so! Yes!' declared Yeshe. He took a step back from Gory and went to sit down, but Great-aunt Millie pulled the chair away just in time to stop him crushing it and he ended up on the floor.

'And Missus Bliss,' Yeshe went on, 'she wonderful person.'

I looked round to see who might want to correct Yeshe on this point, but nobody opened their mouths. Well, Yeshe was a big fella and it seemed as if he'd got some more stuff to get off his chest.

'Missus Bliss,' Yeshe said, 'she nice to me. 'She say if Tiffany ever get husband she like him to be kind and handsome like me.'

I shuddered.

Great-aunt Millie was busily dialling on her mobile.

'Who are you ringing, Great-aunt Millie?' asked Scarlet.

'Yeshe's folk, back in Tibet,' said Great-aunt Millie. 'Just to let them know that Yeshe's not shy any more and is well on the way to becoming a proper monster from the dark side.'

'Good!' said Yeshe. 'And now that snow come, I like sleep outside in garden.'

Brilliant! I'd get my room back!

We all helped Great-aunt Millie put up half a dozen of the Brownies' tents to make a cosy shelter for Yeshe.

When I got home I found Grandad in a gloomy mood.

'Are you all right, Grandad?' I asked.

'Your gran's left us,' he said with a sad sigh.

And then I knew just who the latest woman was that Grandad had fallen in love with: Gran! He handed me a letter:

Dear Jonathan

I have decided to go take a trip to South America. Between you and me, I reckon your mum and dad will need a hand with Ant and Deb's chicks. I should imagine that young penguins are a bit of a handful.

I have enjoyed my stay at Drac's Cottage. The coffin was very comfy. I shall suggest to your mum and dad that they name one of Ant and Deb's baby penguins Keith, after your grandad.

See you again (though I may be in disguise)

Lots of Love

Gran xxx

PS I helped myself to some egg and chips before I left. Tell your grandad the tomato ketchup tasted very funny.

Chapter 21

NEXT MORNING I went round to Scarlet's with Yeshe's bags. The rest of the Fang Gang were already there. Mrs Bliss – and Yeshe – were all over the front pages of the papers and the TV news channels.

Daily Wail
TOP JOURNO (39) ARRESTED AFTER RESCUE BY HUNKY HERO (15)

'Do you think the police will realise they've got the wrong woman?' asked Scarlet.

'With a bit of luck, they won't,' said Gory. He wouldn't have said such a thing in front of Yeshe, of course, but Yeshe was still asleep in the garden.

'I think they will,' I said.

'How can you be so sure?' asked Griselda.

'Because I told them,' I replied.

'You what!' shouted Gory. 'You're as bad as that dopey Yeshe out there. Don't you see we'd be rid of Mrs Bliss for years, if they thought she was a dangerous escaped criminal?'

'And if that were to happen, who do you think would be camping out in my grandad's front room?' I asked. 'Tiffany! That's why I rang the police with an anonymous tip-off. Mrs Bliss will be out of prison by the end of the day hopefully and Tiffany won't be hanging about Drac's Cottage any more.'

Yeshe rolled out of his tents at about midday and we all had a Fang Gang lunch together. He was all smiles.

'I am no longer mouse, but monster!' he declared.

We all clapped and cheered. Then we all sang:

'*For he's a jolly good yeti*
For he's a jolly good yeti
And he's no longer sweaty!
And so say all of us!'

'I ask Mr and Missus Moon if I can stay week and they say yes!'

'In that case, I think we should make Yeshe an honorary member of the Fang Gang,' said Scarlet.

'Here, here!' agreed Griselda. 'All those in favour, raise their hands.'

We all raised our hands, even Gory, although to be technically correct his hand was raised by Scarlet and Griselda, who had grabbed hold of it for him.

'Thank you,' said Yeshe. 'I like. You are nice people Fang Gang. But Mrs Bliss, she also nice—'

'Hey, man, hold it there!' said Crombie the Zombie.

'All those in favour of banning the mention of Mrs Bliss's name, raise your hands,' I said.

We all raised our hands.

After lunch, I helped Scarlet and Great-aunt Millie clear away.

'I noticed that Yeshe's feet still pong,' I said.

Great-aunt Millie nodded.

'Will he *ever* change his socks?' asked Scarlet.

'Oh, give it a couple of years or so,' said Great-aunt Millie.

'A couple of years or so!' I said, amazed. 'Is it a particular yeti problem, not wanting to change your socks?'

'Oh, Yeshe's refusal to change his socks has nothing to do with him being a yeti,' said Great-aunt Millie.

'No?'

'No! The reason Yeshe won't change his socks is because he's a teenager! That's why I said give it a couple of years or so.'

Chapter 22

A WEEK LATER, we all went with Yeshe in the Brownies' minibus to the airport. We were all saying goodbye to him at the check-in when a familiar voice caught our ears:

'Tiffany poppet, do hurry along! We don't want to miss the flight, do we?'

Round the corner came Mrs Bliss, in a wheelchair. Pushing her was a rather breathless and red-faced Tiffany.

Gory, Griselda, Scarlet, Crombie and I all dived out of the way behind the nearest burly security guard. Yeshe, though, called out to Mrs Bliss.

'Missus Bliss. Is me! Yeshe!'

Tiffany leapt out from behind her mum's wheelchair, flung her arms round Yeshe and gave him a great big sloppy kiss.

'Typical,' muttered Scarlet crossly. 'There's me – and you, Griselda – nice girls from the dark side, both of us, and who gets to snog that gorgeous hunk of a yeti? That soppy, stupid Vampire Slayer in Chief, Tiffany Bliss, that's who!'

'Aaargh!' came a sudden scream from Mrs Bliss. In Tiffany's haste to snog Yeshe, she had forgotten to put the brake on her mum's wheelchair, which was now careering backwards towards the down escalator.

Yeshe took two long, quick strides and grabbed the arm of the wheelchair just as it reached the top step.

'I do not believe it,' muttered Gory through

clenched teeth. 'He's saved her life again! That's the third time in two days!'

'You go ski?' we heard Yeshe ask Mrs Bliss, once she had recovered.

'Oh no, not with my ankle,' said Mrs Bliss. 'No, the travel agents have booked us on to an alternative holiday. We don't know where to, it was the only holiday left with any spare places.'

We watched Yeshe go through the gate for his flight, waving him goodbye from our hiding place.

'Gate thirteen for your flight, madam,' said the check-in girl to Mrs Bliss.

Puffing and panting, Tiffany pushed her mum through gate thirteen.

'I wonder where they're off to,' Scarlet said.

I pointed to the departure board. The gate thirteen destination was just flashing up.

GATE 13
FLIGHT NUMBER DRAC 4545
Drac Airtours to Transylvania

'Oh yes!' laughed Griselda.

We ran through to the observation deck and waved off Yeshe's flight to Tibet. Then we waited for Flight Drac 4545. As it taxied down the runway, I could just make out two terrified figures at one of the windows above the wing. Quite what they were shouting I don't know, but at a guess I would say it was something like:

'Help! Get us off this plane!'

'What are you laughing at, Jonathan?' asked Scarlet,

'That!' I replied, looking up at the window of the plane. 'Mrs Bliss and Tiffany on their way to Transylvania! Don't you think it's funny?'

'Oh yes,' said Scarlet, but she wasn't laughing.

'So why are you looking so serious?' I asked.

'Because I'm thinking of you, Jonathan,' she replied, handing me a note:

The Fang Gang
Emergency Meeting: the
Graveyard. This evening.
Item 1: to deal with Jonathan
for spending all our pocket money
buying a bottle of Sinderella
perfume for Tiffany Bliss.

'Look! I can explain,' I said.

'You will,' replied Scarlet. 'This evening.'

Oh dear. You know, sometimes being a member of the Fang Gang is just so . . . well . . . *complicated*.